Geese Find the Missing Piece

School Time Riddle Rhymes

by Marco and Giulio Maestro
pictures by Giulio Maestro

HarperCollins*Publishers*

HarperCollins®, 📖®, and I Can Read Book®
are registered trademarks of HarperCollins Publishers Inc.

Geese Find the Missing Piece
School Time Riddle Rhymes
Text copyright © 1999 by Marco and Giulio Maestro
Illustrations copyright © 1999 by Giulio Maestro
Printed in the U.S.A. All rights reserved.

Library of Congress Cataloging-in-Publication Data
Maestro, Marco.
 Geese find the missing piece : school time riddle rhymes / by Marco and Giulio
Maestro ; pictures by Giulio Maestro.
    p.   cm. — (An I can read book)
 Summary: Rhyming riddles answer questions about a variety of animals at school.
 ISBN 0-06-026220-6. — ISBN 0-06-026221-4 (lib. bdg.)
 1. Riddles, Juvenile.   2. Animals—Juvenile humor.   3. Schools—Juvenile humor.
[1. Animals—Wit and humor.   2. Schools—Wit and humor.   3. Riddles.   4. Jokes.]
I. Maestro, Giulio.   II. Title.   III. Series.
PN6371.5.M235   1999   98-41513
818'.5402—dc21   CIP
                                                                          AC

1 2 3 4 5 6 7 8 9 10
❖
First Edition

www.harperchildrens.com

Geese Find the
Missing Piece
School Time Riddle Rhymes

Where do polar bears
learn their ABCs?

At a **cool** . . .

school!

What does Polly say to Polly

when they meet at school?

We have the **same** . . .

name.

How do the noisy ducks
play with blocks?

They **stack** while they . . .

quack.

How does Bear make a big mess
at playtime?

He **knocks** down all the . . .

blocks.

How is the puzzle finished?

The **geese** find the missing . . .

piece.

Where can you read lots of words?

Take a **look** in a . . .

book.

What does Penguin use to measure?

She uses a **cooler** . . .

ruler.

Why is Crocodile loud at snack time?

He **crunches** when he . . .

crunch crunch crunch crunch

munches.

What color is strawberry punch?

The **drink** is . . .

pink.

What happens when Lion

spills the juice?

He gets a **stain** on his . . .

mane.

What is Gorilla's favorite flavor?

The **ape** loves . . .

grape.

How do Turtle and Rabbit

get ready for rest time?

Before their **naps**,

they take off their . . .

caps.

Where do kittens rest?

Little **cats** lie down on . . .

mats.

How does the teacher

make two kinds of music?

She **hums** as she . . .

hum

strum

strums.

32

How does the class

take a long walk?

They walk in single **file** for a . . .

mile.

What does Snake

like to do best at recess?

She loves to **glide** down the . . .

slide.

How does Lizard

take his friend for a ride?

He carries **Snail** on his . . .

tail.

Why does the teacher

take his class to the sea?

So he can **teach** at the . . .

beach.

Why does Ladybug

practice writing the alphabet?

So she can make each **letter** . . .

better.

Why is Panda's picture
hard to see?

She uses very **faint** . . .

paint.

How do Hippo and Heron
have fun in art?

They **play** with . . .

clay.

What does the driver

say on the way home?

School

"I'm glad there is no **fuss** on this . . .

Bus

bus!"